Big Winner

Author: Sylvia Taekema

April 11, 2023

In this high-interest accessible novel for middle-grade readers, fourteen-year-old Skye worries about her new friend, Digby, after he shares a big secret.

FORMAT	Paperback	PDF	EPUB
5 x 7.5"	9781459834064	9781459834071	9781459834088
128 PAGES	$10.95		

KEY SELLING POINTS

- A young teen worries about her friend when he reveals he has won the lottery.
- The story explores themes of friendship, compassion and doing the right thing.
- While readers will identify with Skye, the young teen who has had to leave her life behind, Digby, a young man with intellectual challenges, is the heart of this story.
- Enhanced features (dyslexia-friendly font, cream paper, larger trim size) to increase reading accessibility for dyslexic and other striving readers.

ABOUT THE AUTHOR

SYLVIA TAEKEMA'S first novel, *Seconds*, was voted a Silver Birch Express Award Honour Book. She is also the author of the middle-grade novel *Ripple Effect*, as well as *Running Behind* in the Orca Currents line. Sylvia lives in Muskoka, Ontario.

Author photo by Trish Wolting-Meiboom

D1509543

PROMOTIONAL PLANS INCLUDE

- Print and online advertising campaigns
- Promotion at national and regional school, library and trade conferences
- Extensive ARC distribution, including NetGalley
- Blog and social media promotion
- Outreach in Orca newsletters

BISACS

JUV039060   JUVENILE FICTION / Social Themes / Friendship
JUV074000   JUVENILE FICTION / Diversity & Multicultural
JUV039140   JUVENILE FICTION / Social Themes / Self-Esteem & Self-Reliance

RIGHTS

Worldwide

AGES

9–12

Orca Currents are short, high-interest novels with contemporary themes written specifically for middle-school students reading below grade level. Reading levels from grade 2.0 to 5.0.

For more information or a review copy, please contact
Kennedy Cullen at kennedy@orcabook.com

Order online at orcabook.com or orders@orcabook.com or 1-800-210-5277

@orcabook

ORCA BOOK PUBLISHERS
orcabook.com • 1-800-210-5277

BIG
WINNER

BIG WINNER

SYLVIA TAEKEMA

ORCA BOOK PUBLISHERS

Published in Canada and the United States in 2023 by Orca Book Publishers.
orcabook.com

Library and Archives Canada Cataloguing in Publication
Title: Big winner / Sylvia Taekema.
Names: Taekema, Sylvia, 1964- author.
Series: Orca currents.
Description: Series statement: Orca currents
Identifiers: Canadiana (print) 20220242135 | Canadiana (ebook) 20220242216 |
ISBN 9781459834064 (softcover) | ISBN 9781459834071 (PDF) |
ISBN 9781459834088 (EPUB)
Classification: LCC PS8639.A25 B54 2023 | DDC jC813/.6—dc23

Library of Congress Control Number: 2022938543

Summary: In this high-interest accessible novel for
middle-grade readers, fourteen-year-old Skye worries about
her new friend, Digby, after he shares a big secret.

Orca Book Publishers is committed to reducing the consumption of
nonrenewable resources in the production of our books. We make
every effort to use materials that support a sustainable future.

Orca Book Publishers gratefully acknowledges the support for its publishing
programs provided by the following agencies: the Government of Canada,
the Canada Council for the Arts and the Province of British Columbia
through the BC Arts Council and the Book Publishing Tax Credit.

Edited by Tanya Trafford
Design by Ella Collier
Cover artwork by Getty Images/kali9 and Getty Images/filo
Author photo by Trish Wolting-Meiboom

Printed and bound in Canada.

26 25 24 23 • 1 2 3 4

For Michelle, who understands

that sometimes change is tough.

Chapter One

The three little bells jangled when I pushed open the coffee-shop door. But no one noticed. The place was fuller than I'd ever seen it, and it was noisy. I stashed my backpack in the small staff room, washed my hands and hurried out front.

"Hey, Skye," said Digby.

"Hey, Digby. What's going on?"

"Umm. Just the regular. I'm doing sugars right now and then—"

"No, I mean…Digby, this is way more than the regular afternoon coffee crowd. The place is packed. What's up? What's everybody talking about?"

Digby looked out over the seating area. "Oh. Yeah. The whole town is going bonkers."

He went back to filling sugar dispensers. He always stopped exactly when the container was full, and he never spilled. He was a pro. His *Brew-n-Bake* visor sat straight on his brown curls. His bright-green polo shirt was clean and tucked.

I straightened my own shirt. "Bonkers is right. Do you know why?"

Digby held up one hand. His forehead crinkled. "Wait. I need to concentrate."

I waited. Digby finished with the sugar. Then he checked that each of the four coffee pots was full or filling. He put more water on for tea. He made sure the napkin dispensers had enough napkins and the stir-stick containers had enough stir sticks. He did this several times each shift. I should have known better than to talk to him while he was busy. If he got interrupted, he would start his routine all over again. I used to try to help him, but he would just shake his head and wave me away. These were his jobs. Mine were to take orders and work the cash register. The one thing we usually did together was wipe down tables after closing.

I'd been at this job for about a month. I was pretty new to Kentville and wasn't having a lot of luck with the whole making-friends thing at school. Maybe the black hat, black jeans, black jacket and boots thing put them off, but hey, I dressed the way I felt. My mom had been unhappy with her job in Calgary for a while and wanted to come back to Nova Scotia, where she grew up. Don't ask me why. It wasn't like we had any family left down here. To make a terrible idea even worse, she decided we would move during Christmas break. That meant messing up our holiday and destroying my first semester of high school. She had gotten a job as a nurse at one of Kentville's old folks' homes. It was the same place she had volunteered at when she was in high school.

"Isn't that great?" she had said. "It's like it's meant to be. It's like coming back home."

I didn't know about that. To me it felt like going backward instead of moving forward. She said I should find a place to volunteer at, but I didn't have time. I was too busy feeling sorry for myself. I knew that's what I was doing, but I didn't care. I had no interest in changing things. I'd been through enough change already.

Coming east meant I'd had to leave my friends. I'd had to leave my best hang-out spots. I'd had to leave a steady babysitting job for the world's sweetest two-year-old. Worst of all, my brother Cade hadn't come with us in the move. He was in his first year of a cooking program that was really hard to get into. He didn't want to give that up. Or his part-time job. Or his Thursday-night hockey games. He didn't want to come to Kentville. I got that. I didn't want to either. But I was only fourteen, so I didn't get to choose.

On the day we left, Cade messed up my hair. I hated when he did that. "Going to miss me, Nerd Girl?" he asked.

"Not one bit," I said, punching him on the arm. But it wasn't true. Not one bit.

"It'll be okay, Skye," Mom said after we'd hugged Cade one more time and pulled away for the long drive east. "You'll see. I know you'll miss your brother, but he's just getting started on his own life. And we've got an adventure ahead. We'll chat with Cade whenever we can."

"It won't be the same," I'd grumbled as I stared out the window.

"Just give it a chance," Mom had said. "You'll like it."

So far it wasn't that great, never mind what spin Mom tried to put on it. She loved the little house we'd bought in Kentville. "Isn't it cute?" she said. "Isn't it cozy? It has so much more character than the one we had in Calgary."

By character, I guess she meant this one was about a thousand years older. It had tiny closets and creaky floors. What she was forgetting was, character or not, that house in Calgary was my home. And I wanted it back. But I didn't tell her how I felt. I showed her. I went out to the mall on the last few days of Christmas break. I had my hair dyed black with blue tips. I bought myself a whole new wardrobe—all black. I thought my mom would be angry about it when I got back, but she didn't say a thing. She just asked me if I had finished unpacking the boxes in my room and what we should have for dinner.

What Mom did say more than once over the next few weeks were things like, "Honestly, Skye.

Of all the things to forget to bring from Calgary! You forgot to pack your smile. And it was such a nice one too." She would make faces at me from the tiny kitchen table where she sat drinking tea in the mornings, trying to make me laugh. She always wore pink scrubs. Or tops with daisies or bright-yellow happy faces all over them. She was trying hard, and I loved her for it. But I wasn't ready to forgive her. So I just tugged my black knit hat down a little farther, put on my boots and left for school.

School was school. I muddled through the end of the first semester and then started the second. Math. English. Science. Geography. The teachers were okay. Since they didn't seem to expect much of a kid who looked like me, I didn't give them much in return. Students had already formed their friend groups, and the special status I'd had being the new kid wore off in about three days. There was one girl, Lainey, who tried harder than the rest. She didn't seem to mind when I didn't answer her questions or when I didn't get excited about the news she shared. I knew I was being a twit, but I didn't have the energy to be nice to her. She was probably great, but she wasn't Cara or Lindsay or Melinda. Those were my friends back home. Or used to be.

We had texted a lot at first. All during my big trip, they'd asked to see the sights going east. I'd just sent them photos of the highway and telephone poles and gas stations. I didn't hear much from Cara and Lindsay anymore. I figured they were getting tired of the black mood. Or their lives had just closed over the hole I'd left. Mel hung in the longest. The last time she called, I told her living in Kentville was the worst.

She laughed and said, "It can't be that bad."

"How do you know? You're not here."

Her voice went soft. "Maybe if you just tried, Skye?"

"Don't you think I am trying?" I'd said it louder than I meant to. Mel didn't say anything right away, and I got mad and ended the call. I hadn't heard from her since. Nobody seemed to care about anything I felt. Or did. Or didn't do. Well then, I thought, why should I? I decided I would cut all ties. I would make no commitments. I would spend most of my time in my room. I thought this would mean freedom and that it would make me feel better, but it didn't. I was lonely. That's when I started coming to the coffee shop.

Chapter Two

My mom worked a lot of afternoon shifts. I didn't love coming home to an empty house in the early-winter dark. All those unfamiliar, unexpected creaks—it was spooky. Walking down the slushy sidewalk one day after school, I saw the sign for *CD's Brew-n-Bake*. So I went in. The place was bright and clean. There were half a dozen customers. It smelled like coffee and cinnamon. The trays by the counter were filled with all kinds of delicious-looking baked goods. And it was warm. I started stopping in every afternoon. Sometimes I'd order a coffee or a hot chocolate, but most times I didn't have any money with me. I had spent my babysitting stash on my hair and new clothes, and I was pretty much broke. I just sat and listened to the buzz of conversations around me. I finished all the homework I never planned to hand in and started writing stories on the back pages of my notebooks. Somehow it was easier to write at the shop than in my room. I was comfortable there.

One afternoon the lady who I guessed ran the place came up to my table. She had short gray hair. Her name tag said *Cheryl*. She looked like a no-nonsense sort of person. I thought for sure she was going to ask me to leave. She would probably say I had to buy something if I wanted to sit at a table. Or maybe she didn't like kids with blue-tipped hair and black hats hanging around in her shop. "Do you mind?" she asked, pointing to the chair across from me.

I shook my head. "Please," I squeaked. I cleared my throat. "Have a seat."

"Thanks." She sighed and stretched her legs out under the table. "Ahhh. That's better. My feet are killing me. I'm Cheryl. Cheryl Lyons. Me and Denny—that's my husband—we own the place. It was always a dream of ours to have our own coffee shop. When we both retired from our jobs in Halifax, we decided to give it a shot."

"It's a nice place," I said. "And everything looks delicious."

"Oh, thanks, hon. Denny's got a real knack for that sort of thing. He bakes, and I take care of the early-morning coffee drinkers. Then the midmorning crowd. Then Digby—you know Digby?"

I nodded. I assumed he must be the big guy in the green shirt who I always saw checking the sugar dispensers, filling doughnut trays or sweeping the floor. He worked hard. One time he gave me a gigantic carrot muffin, no charge.

"He comes every day at noon and helps until six, when we close. We've only been at this since the new year, but we've got a bunch of regular customers already. Business is steady. It was a lot of hard work to get going, let me tell you. But now that the place seems to have taken off, me and Denny would like to be able to knock off by three or four every day."

I nodded. I was unsure why she was telling me all this.

"We've seen you in here quite a bit."

Uh-oh. Here it comes, I thought. I gulped.

"We're wondering if you would consider coming in after school. Digby's such a gem. You couldn't ask for a better employee. He keeps the place so clean it sparkles. And he's great with the customers. But he doesn't like anything to do with numbers. So we need someone to look after the cash register.

It'd be every day after school until closing. My niece, Nicole, is up at the university during the week, but she takes care of the weekends for us. What do you think, Skye? Are you interested?"

She was offering me a job? I was surprised. I was still waiting for the moment she was going to ask me to order a hot chocolate or be on my way. I nodded slowly. "How did you know my name?"

"Skye Richardson, right? Digby told me. He's the one who recommended you. He said he saw your name on your notebook. He said he sees you doing math homework a lot, so he knows you must be good at numbers. He also said he likes the blue tips on your hair. He thinks you must have chosen blue because your name is Skye."

Huh. Math homework I didn't always hand in and blue hair. Interesting recommendation.

"Oh, and he said you looked happy. Just the type to work with people."

I almost snorted out loud at that but managed to cover it up by clearing my throat. And then I accepted Cheryl's offer. I had just started thinking about how I could earn my own money. Maybe a babysitting gig. This was even better. Her timing was perfect. Plus, the job would give me a reason to come to the shop after school without having to hide out.

Cheryl grinned. "Great!" she said. She got up from her chair and hurried to the back. When she returned, she handed me a black polo shirt with the *CD's Brew-n-Bake* logo on it. And a bright-green one like Digby's. That was wishful thinking on her part, I thought. It was obvious I wore only black.

Cheryl looked me up and down. "I can see you're pretty attached to that hat."

I nodded. Was she going to ask me to change my look?

She smiled. "So I figure you won't need the visor."

I started the next day. And quickly found out what working with Digby Jones was like.

Chapter Three

Digby was…Digby. He was super serious about his job. He was really good at it and was patient at showing me what to do. I found out, though, that I had to stick to my jobs or he'd get annoyed. If I interrupted him during his, he got frustrated. But I figured out pretty quickly what to do and what not to do. We got along great. Most of the time he was super friendly. He knew every customer, and every customer knew him. He took great care, making their orders just the way they liked them. I felt sort of small working beside him, and it wasn't just because he was so tall. He had a presence. I didn't know exactly how to put it into words.

"A-plus," said Digby, snapping me out of my thoughts.

"What?"

"Everything looks A-plus. All the containers are full. There's lots of coffee ready. What were you asking me, Skye?"

"Oh. Right." I swept an arm out toward the buzzing crowd. "There's a lot of people here today. Do you know what they're talking about? Everyone seems super excited about something."

Digby grinned. "They're all talking about the lottery ticket. Somebody won a million dollars, and whoever has the winning ticket bought it right here in Kentville. At the convenience store. Mr. Lemsky showed me the story in the newspaper. He showed me the numbers." Digby looked up at the ceiling as if the numbers were pasted there. He crinkled his forehead. "Ten, twenty-one, four, twenty-eight, seven, sixteen."

"A million dollars?" I asked. "Wowzers. I bet everybody's trying to remember if they bought a ticket. Or where they might have put it. You think it's someone who actually lives in Kentville? What do you think they'll do with all that money?"

Digby laughed. "That's what everybody's talking about."

"A million dollars. Whoo-ee." I took a deep breath and looked out over the crowd again. "It's like a fever, isn't it? A frenzy. Delirium. That's the word for this."

Digby smiled. "Delirium. That's a good word. You always come up with the best ones, Skye."

I really did like words. I collected them. Every now and then I'd slip a new one into the conversation. Or into one of my stories. I had added *gobsmacked* to my word list not too long ago and was waiting for the perfect occasion to use it. I liked having the right word at the right time. Except I couldn't come up with the right word for what Digby said next. In fact, I couldn't come up with any words at all.

He was shaking his head. "Yeah. Delirium. Frenzy. Fever." Then he leaned down and whispered to me, "I have it."

Now I was the one with the crinkled forehead. I looked at him. "You have what, Digby? A fever?" I stepped back.

He shook his head. "The ticket."

"What ticket?"

"The ticket everyone is talking about."

I stared at him. "What do you mean? Did you buy a lottery ticket?"

"No, nope, uh-uh." He shook his head. "Aunt Amy, she told me never to buy lottery tickets. 'They're just a pure waste of money,' she said.

Especially with the kind of luck I have. She always told me, 'You just work hard and save your money, Digs, and pretty soon you'll have a nice tidy little sum without counting on that kind of nonsense.'"

I smiled. I couldn't help it. Though I'd never met her, I could just hear Digby's aunt talking. "Well then, what ticket do you have?"

"I told you. The winning lottery ticket."

I sighed. "But you just said you don't buy lottery tickets."

"I didn't buy it. Uncle Joey did. And then he gave it to me. He said to keep it in my wallet. When I heard people talking about the winning ticket and Mr. Lemsky showed me the numbers, I thought, well, those are the same ones."

"You have a ticket with those numbers on it?" I didn't know if Digby was for real. After all, he had said himself numbers weren't his thing. "Can you show me?"

Digby shook his head. "Not now, Skye. Are you kidding? We're in the middle of a shift. Look at all these people."

"Okay, you're right. When we get a break then?"

Digby nodded. "If we get a break today." He shooed me over to the cash register, where a lineup had begun to form.

"Right now we have more coffee to serve, Skye. And hot chocolate and tea. And doughnuts."

"You're right, Digby. First things first." But wow, a million dollars? What would I do with that? Buy our old house back and move home! Or maybe buy a different house in Calgary to make Mom happy. One with character. I'd be back with Cade and Cara and Lindsay and Mel. But we'd fly back, of course. I didn't want to be squished in with all our stuff like when we drove out to Kentville. With that kind of money, we could buy all new stuff. And then maybe we'd fly some more. To Los Angeles. Or Hawaii. Or Greece. A million dollars! I had a hard time concentrating on orders.

Chapter Four

Digby was right. We didn't get a break. But when all those people finally went home and we finished cleaning up, Digby showed me his ticket. Sure enough, the numbers matched. Well, five of them did. The last one was half-covered by a brown smudge.

"What is that? Coffee?"

Digby peered at the ticket. He shook his head. "Probably chocolate. Uncle Joey loved chocolate."

"But Digby—the last lottery number was a sixteen. With the chocolate smudge, how do you know for sure this is a sixteen? It could be something else."

"Easy. The numbers start with ten and twenty-one, right? That's October 21, Aunt Amy's birthday. The next two numbers are four and twenty-eight." He counted on his fingers. "January, February, March, April. Four twenty-eight is April 28. That's Aunt Amy and Uncle Joey's anniversary. I know because Uncle Joey always said, 'April 28 is a very important date,' so he wouldn't forget. Every April 28 he made a big deal about bringing Aunt Amy flowers and a box of chocolates. She liked the flowers, but he ate the chocolate because, you know, she was diabetic."

"Okay, but what about the last two?"

"Well, that's seven and sixteen. That's July 16, and that's Uncle Joey's birthday. It was always easy to remember, because his birthday's two days before mine. Whenever it was his birthday, he would tease me about having to wait."

"But how can you be *sure* that's a six?"

"Look, you can see the bottom half of the number, and you can see it's a circle. This is for sure the number six. July 16 was Uncle Joey's birthday, and sixteen was always his lucky number. This is the ticket Uncle Joey bought. These were the three most important dates for him. So I know those are the numbers."

I let out a long, slow breath. "Okay, but there's one more thing, Digby. Your uncle signed it. See, look here. It says *J. Jones*, for Joey Jones."

Digby peered at the ticket again. "No. It's *J* for John."

"Who's John?"

"Uncle Joey. His real name was John."

"So how can you claim the ticket then if he has signed it?"

"I signed it. My name is John too."

I shook my head. "What do you mean your name is John too? Your name is Digby."

"No, my name is John. Everybody in my family is named John. Well, not the girls, of course. They are Brenna and Lauren and Ava and Kim and—"

I didn't know how many relatives Digby had, but it seemed like he might never stop. "But all the boys are named John?"

"Well, no, there's Pete and David and Lenny and Neil—"

"No, no, you said something about the name John?"

"Every family has a John. We're named after my great-great-gazillionth grandpa or something. The oldest boy in the family is always named John. Tradition is really important in my family. But having that many Johns gets confusing, so sometimes we call them by their dad's name. Like, Uncle Harold's John is Harry, and Uncle Martin's John is Marty."

"And Joseph's John was Joey?"

"No, there's no Joseph. Uncle Joey just liked being called Joey better than John."

I thought about this for a minute. "So…your dad's name was Digby?"

He shook his head. "That's not a name."

"What do you mean it's not a name? It's your name, isn't it?"

"Yes, but…no." He shook his head. "It's just… nobody knows my dad's name. Not even me. They called me Digby John because that's where I was born. In the town of Digby. It's about an hour west of here. People just call me Digby now."

"So if the ticket is signed *J. Jones*, that's you?"

"Yep. Uncle Joey told me to use my official name when I signed the ticket so no one could take it away from me. I guess he knew he might…"

Digby's voice cracked. His face began to crumple. Cheryl had told me that Digby's uncle Joey had died of a heart attack a few months back.

It was just two weeks after his aunt Amy had died from complications due to diabetes. According to Digby, Joey had died of a broken heart because he was so sad after he lost his wife. They had been married for fifty-seven years. Digby had lived with them since he was four years old. That's when his mom, Leann, had left Nova Scotia to look for work. She had died in a motorcycle accident in Ontario not long after. Poor Digby. He didn't know who his dad was. His mom had died. Now the two people who had raised him and loved him the longest were gone too.

I held up the ticket. "Hey, Digby, listen. If this is your signature, do you know what this ticket means?"

"Uh-huh." He took a deep breath. "I have a lot of money."

"And aren't you happy about that?"

His green eyes were about to spill over. "I miss Uncle Joey."

"I know you do. But this is an awesome gift Uncle Joey gave you. This little piece of paper is worth a *million* dollars." I was getting hotter and hotter just thinking about it, so warm I almost took off my hat. And I never took off my hat. Except for when I went to sleep at night, and not even always then. "Have you thought about what you are going to do with that?"

Digby grabbed a napkin and blew his nose. His mouth was a firm line. "I can't think about that yet."

"You have to claim it."

"Claim it?"

"Show the numbers to someone official and then ask for the money."

He shook his head. "No, not yet. And you can't tell anybody about the ticket, okay? Not yet. I haven't made my list."

"What list?"

"Of the things I need to get. Of the things I need to do. I need to get that done first. You're good at math, Skye. Will you help me?"

A list. That was a good idea. It would be good for Digby to think things through so he wouldn't blow all the money at once. I heard a lot of winners did that. Digby probably had a little bit of time before he had to claim the money. It would be okay to keep this a secret until he was ready. And he was smiling again. Good. He seemed to have calmed down. My heart, meanwhile, was still beating wildly. This was nuts! A million dollars. I couldn't stop thinking about what to do with all that money, and it wasn't even mine.

Chapter Five

The next afternoon at the shop, just the regular crowd was in. I found Digby behind the counter as usual. "Hey, Big Winner," I said quietly. "I've been looking into this lottery-ticket thing. You have up to a year to claim the prize, but you have to be eighteen. Are you eighteen?"

Digby nodded. "I'm eighteen. I'll be nineteen in July. July 18. I liked turning eighteen on the eighteenth. This time I'll just have to be nineteen, I guess."

"Right." I watched him as he fit a few more mugs into the dishwasher and started it up. "Digby, did you…where did you go to school?"

"I went to Aldershot Elementary from kindergarten to eighth grade. Then in high school I was in Mrs. Flynn's life-skills class, which was the best thing ever. She helped me get my job at Boston Pizza. I liked working there. Everyone was super nice. Then Cheryl hired me. I really, really like working here. It's great because Denny is always giving me muffins and doughnuts and stuff for free. And I can walk here from the group home, which is where I live now since Aunt Amy and Uncle Joey…"

Uh-oh. I jumped in to distract him. "Hey! So you are old enough to claim the ticket. Digby, you'll be rich. You can buy your own house now. A big fancy one."

He shook his head. "Uh-uh. I like my room at the group home. We've got foosball and a Ping-Pong table, plus we have internet and TV. I can watch all my favorite shows."

"What about a bigger-screen TV then, just for you?"

"The one at the group home is big. And we all watch it together. I like that. I'm not allowed to watch it before work, because that's when we do our chores, but I can watch it after work."

"But you won't have to work anymore if you're rich. You can retire."

"What do you mean?"

"You know, quit your job and take it easy every day. Just do what you want."

"Why would I do that? I like my job. I'm already doing what I want."

"Oh." I tried again. "Well then, what about a vacation?"

Digby's eyes lit up. "A vacation? Yeah, I would like that."

"Now you're talking. Where would you go? A world tour? A cruise? The Caribbean? Paris? The pyramids?"

Digby grinned. "I know, I know." He closed his eyes and drew in a deep breath, like he was envisioning the most wonderful place on earth. Then he looked me in the eye and said, "I would like to go to Halifax for a day. A whole day."

I stared at him. "Halifax?" Was he kidding? The city was barely an hour's drive from here.

"Yeah. For a whole day. I've never been there. Uncle Joey didn't like to drive in too much traffic, and I didn't want to go by myself on the bus. I'd go to see...whatever there is to see there...and then I'd have a special dinner." He looked up at the ceiling for a moment. "At KFC. That's my favorite." He looked over at me. "Wouldn't that be a great day, Skye?"

Like my mother, Digby seemed to have some strange ideas about what kinds of things were awesome. "Sounds great, Digby."

The bells on the door jangled. "Look, here comes Mr. Davey for his usual black coffee. And probably a blueberry muffin, warmed up, no butter," said Digby. "We better get to work. Maybe tomorrow you can help me with my list."

"Sure."

Chapter Six

The next day was Saturday. Digby had asked me to meet him at the coffee shop at nine. "No way," I said. "On Saturdays I don't crawl out of my cave until eleven."

When he asked me what cave, I told him it meant I liked to sleep in and wouldn't be awake that early. He frowned but agreed to the later time.

As I walked over, I thought about all the things I would put on a list if I were writing one for myself. First I'd buy my old life back. Then I'd make it even better. I'd buy a big house. I'd buy a car, even though I wouldn't be able to drive it yet. I could hire a driver. A chauffeur. How cool would that be? And maybe a jet. My own jet. And I'd get some expensive jewelry, although I didn't really like wearing jewelry. And fancy clothes, as long as that didn't mean giving up my all-black fashion lineup. Maybe I'd buy books. Tons and tons of books. And food. Like pizza. Lots and lots of pizza. And a lifetime supply of Swedish Berries. And Sour Cherry Blasters. And wine gums. Maybe I'd buy entire candy factories. And restaurants. I'd buy one for Cade. He could be the chef, and I could have fantastic parties. I'd have to ask Mel what she thought. Then I remembered that I wasn't talking to Mel. And Cade hadn't called even once. I missed him messing up my hair. I missed him calling me

Nerd Girl. No doubt he was too busy with his own great life to think about mine. Then I remembered I had decided not to care.

Digby was waiting for me when I pushed through the door at eleven fifteen. He was sitting at a table by the window. In front of him were two steaming mugs and two doughnuts. He had a piece of paper in his hand that he kept unfolding and refolding. There were maybe a dozen other people in the shop.

"Skye!" Digby said when I sat down across from him. His smile was as wide as ever. "I got you some coffee to help you wake up. And a doughnut! With sprinkles!"

"Hey, Digby. Thanks. Sprinkles are the best." I shrugged off my coat. "Doesn't it feel weird to be sitting here instead of being behind the counter?"

"Yes. Nicole won't let me back there. I had to sit on my hands so I wouldn't go fill the doughnut trays. Some people don't do it right."

Nicole looked over and rolled her eyes, but she was smiling. I waved to her.

"Don't we have another job to do anyway, Digby?" I said, turning back to him. "What about this list of yours?"

"Right," he said. I could tell he was nervous but also really excited. And I had to admit, I was pretty excited for him. He unfolded the paper he'd been holding. He smoothed it out and slid it across the table to me. Here it was. A list of how to spend his money. I don't know what I was expecting. But it wasn't this. This wasn't a list of things. It was a list of names.

Digby took a deep breath, leaned toward me and said quietly, "I want to add some things to my list, but I need to know how much they cost. First of all, Mrs. Lee wants to go to Toronto to visit her grandkids. In July, when they're out of school. How much would that be, for her to get there?"

I looked at him. "Mrs. Lee? Why—"

"How much, Skye?"

I pulled out my phone and looked it up. "Halifax to Toronto?"

He nodded.

"And back?"

He nodded again.

"And maybe some spending money?"

"Oh, that's a good idea. I didn't think of that."

"That would be about $700."

"Okay. Can you write that down here?" He reached over and pointed to the space behind Mrs. Lee's name on the piece of paper.

I wrote it down.

"Good. Now Tim Birch wants to buy a new bike for Lexie for her birthday."

"Who's Lexie?"

"His daughter. She's turning nine."

"But what—"

"Where could we get a bike for her, Skye?" Digby looked at me earnestly.

"I don't know. Walmart, maybe? She's nine?"

"Turning nine," he corrected. "Tim's wife, Annie, is really mad at him about something, and Tim is living by himself in an apartment. He wants to give Lexie something really nice for her birthday. We need to find a bike, Skye."

I googled kids' bikes and showed the pictures to Digby.

His forehead crinkled. "Which one, do you think?"

"What if you get him a gift card? Then he can pick one out himself."

Digby beamed. "Yes!" he shouted. His cheeks flushed pink as he looked around the shop. He started whispering again. "And we need enough for a helmet too, right? How much do you think for a bike and a helmet, Skye?"

"Ummm, $200 should do it."

He pointed at the piece of paper again. "Okay. Put that here."

"Done."

He sat back and closed his eyes. "Okay. The next one is a big number. I need to pay for a new roof for the Dubrovskys. I talked to Mr. Todd Matthews of Matthews' Roofing and Siding. He went to have a look, and he told me about $6,500 would do it. They don't have a very big house, and that seems like a lot of money. But I know Mr. Matthews wouldn't tell me the wrong amount. Mr. and Mrs. Dubrovsky want to sell their house and move into an apartment, but they can't sell it for what they want for it if the roof leaks. Can you put $6,500 on the list beside their name, please, Skye?"

"Yes, but why would you pay for their roof repairs, Digby?"

"Because they need them."

"But—"

He held up one hand. "Wait. I'm not done. I need to concentrate. Mrs. McGrady needs a new stove at the soup kitchen."

I fiddled with my phone again and then turned it to show Digby. "Stu's Appliances, on sale, $850. What do you think?"

"Oooh, that's nice. Does it have good reviews? Aunt Amy always told me to look at the reviews before I buy something."

I did some scrolling. "Four and a half stars."

Digby nodded. "That's pretty good. Write it down."

I had just added the zero to $850 when someone slid onto the chair beside me.

"Hey there, Digby!"

"Nate! How are you doing?"

"Pretty good, buddy. I haven't seen you in a while."

Digby pointed in my direction. "This is Skye."

I nodded, even though Digby didn't say anything about who this guy was. Nate looked me up and down and then smirked. Guess my clothes and hair didn't impress him. But what did I care what this guy thought? He didn't know me. And I didn't think I really wanted to know him. There was something about him I didn't like.

Nate turned back to Digby. "What's up, big guy? I couldn't really help overhearing…" He lowered his voice and leaned in. "Did you come into some money lately?"

"Ummm, yes."

Nate sucked in his breath. "You don't happen to have a certain lottery ticket, do you?"

"A lottery ticket?" Digby asked.

"A winning lottery ticket?"

I cleared my throat, hoping Digby would look over at me shaking my head. I didn't know if Digby should be telling Nate about his big win. As far as I knew, he hadn't told anybody yet except me.

I was about to kick Digby under the table when he answered. "Ummm, Nate, I can't talk about that now. I need to talk to Skye about the park."

"The park?"

"The one by Uncle Joey's. It needs, it needs—"

"Oakview? I know that park. It needs a lot of things." Nate's eyes were bright, and he was talking fast. "Are you planning to upgrade that park, Digby? With some of your money?"

"Money? Yes, no…" Digby was getting agitated. "Skye is helping me make my list. I can't talk now, Nate."

"Sure, Digby. I get it. You have lots to think about. But the park is definitely on your list?"

"On my list." Digby nodded.

"What do you think of putting a skate park at Oakview? Wouldn't that be great? Town council's been talking about that forever, but no one's ever done anything about it."

Digby's eyes lit up. "A skate park? A skate park would be awesome. I would love to have a skate park."

"Yeah? Cool. Hey, do you think it would be okay if I took your picture? Then I'll get out of your way and won't bother you one more second."

"My picture?"

"Yeah. We're buddies, aren't we? I'd like to have a picture of my buddy."

"Okay. Sure."

I was still shaking my head, but Digby just smiled his huge smile for Nate. I didn't like it. Something about this guy made me uneasy. "Wait." I grabbed Nate's wrist so he couldn't aim his phone. "Digby, how do you and Nate know each other? Is he a friend of yours?"

"Nate? Sure. He goes to my school. Or he still goes, I guess. I'm done. I am a working man now." Digby grinned. "Nate took our picture for the yearbook when our life-skills class made lasagna for the community dinner. And when we handed out bottles of water to everyone during the Terry Fox Run. And when we helped make the mats out of plastic bags for people who needed them to sleep on. And when—"

"Okay, okay." I got it. Digby's class did cool stuff, and Nate liked taking pictures. That made me feel a little bit better. It wasn't like the photo was going to end up on the news or anything. "You're not going to share this picture all over your social media, are you?" I asked Nate.

Nate smiled a slow smile. "All over my social media? No. Who are you, the photo police?" Nate took the picture. "Thanks, big guy! Great to meet you, Skye." He turned and left the cafe. Good riddance, I thought.

Chapter Seven

Nicole came over and picked up our empty cups. "Need anything else?" she asked as she wiped the table.

"You missed a spot," said Digby.

Nicole peered at the table. "Where?"

"And did you fill the napkin dispensers?" asked Digby. "Are the stir-stick containers full?"

"You are not working today, Digby. Let me look after the place."

"But—"

Nicole threatened to throw her dishcloth at him. I tapped the list. "I didn't know you were a skateboarder, Digby," I said, hoping to get him back on task.

"I'm not a skateboarder."

"But you said you would love a skate park at Oakview."

He shook his head. "I just like to watch. Some kids can do some pretty cool tricks. Aunt Amy told me never to get one of those things. She always said, 'Digby, you'll break your head open, and what will we do then? You've only got the one.'"

We both laughed. It felt good. I realized that it was getting harder and harder to maintain my gloomy outlook in this town.

"What was it you were going to tell me about the park then, Digby, before Nate interrupted?"

"The park?"

"For your list."

"Oh yeah!" He was smiling again. "I need you to write this number beside Aunt Amy and Uncle Joey's names. One, five, zero, zero. With a dollar sign."

I wrote $1,500 behind Uncle Joey's name. "Like this?"

"Yes."

"What's it for?"

"It's a surprise."

"That's a big surprise."

"Yep. And I'm not going to tell you what it is." His eyes twinkled, and he pretended to lock his lips together and throw away the key.

"Okay, well, what else?"

"Does that add up to $10,000 yet, Skye?"

I did a quick crunch of the numbers. "Pretty close."

"Over or under?"

"A little bit under."

"Okay, good." He looked at the paper. "I wanted to get something for Olivia Williams, but I don't know what."

"What's going on with Olivia?"

"Someone keeps calling her bad names at school."

"Hmmm. I don't know if there's anything you can buy to fix that."

"Maybe I'll buy her a doughnut next time she comes in. Strawberry-filled. That seems right."

I smiled just a little. "That sounds like a nice thing to do, Digby. Why does this person call her bad names?"

"I don't know. I can't think of any reason at all."

"Lots of people do mean things for no good reason, Digby."

"Not Olivia. She is always nice to me. She never leaves crumbs on her table, and she always brings her mug to the counter before she leaves the shop. And not Nicole or Denny or Cheryl or you either, Skye. Thanks for helping me with my list. You're a good friend. The best."

I had to say, he caught me off guard with that one. My throat got a little tight. "No problem, Digby. I just added up a few numbers, that's all. Anything else?"

He shook his head. I was glad. Ten thousand dollars was a lot of money, but at least he wasn't blowing the whole million. "How do you know all these people need these things?"

"They say things. When they get their coffee and doughnuts. I listen."

"Yeah, but they're not asking you to get these things for them, are they, Digby? They're just talking about them to their friends, right? I'm just, I want, I'm wondering...are you actually going to buy all this stuff?"

"Of course."

"Why don't…why don't you use your money to get some things that will make *you* happy?"

He stared at me. "What do you mean? I already am happy."

Chapter Eight

By Tuesday the million-dollar secret was out. Digby hadn't said another word. Neither had I. It was Nate. I knew I'd been right to feel uneasy about him. I should have asked more questions. As promised, he didn't share Digby's picture on his personal social media. He just posted it on the *Kings County Register* Facebook page and on the front page of the *Register* itself. It didn't take up a lot of space, but the headline and the story that went with it sure had a huge impact.

Ticket to treasure?

This reporter has learned that a local coffee-shop worker may soon stop handing out doughnuts and start making donations. Digby Jones, an employee at CD's Brew-n-Bake, may just have the winning ticket in a recent lottery draw. He might be planning to use some of his windfall to restore Oakview Park. This is something town council has been putting off for years. Rumor has it that a skate park could even be part of the plan. If this much-needed renewal happens, council should consider changing the name of the park in honor of such a generous donor.

—Nate Frazer, special to the Kings County Register

The coffee shop was buzzing again. Everyone was asking Digby about the ticket and teasing him about sharing the money with them. Cheryl had stayed to help handle the crowd and keep an eye on things. She was the one who filled me in on what had happened. She showed me a copy of the *Register*. One of the dozen or so that were making their way around the coffee shop.

"*May* have the winning ticket? *Might* be planning? *Rumor?* How did this get in here?" I asked. "This isn't good journalism."

"You're right about that, young lady." Mr. Lemsky, editor of the *Register*, was standing on the other side of the counter. He looked grumpy. "Cheryl, I'm sorry, I can see you're busy, but may I talk to Digby for a few minutes?"

"Sure, David. Skye, take Mr. Lemsky to the staff room in the back, would you? I'll send Digby over. And you stay too, okay, Skye? Digby could use a friend by his side right now. I'll handle things up here."

I wanted to tell Cheryl I didn't really do the friends thing anymore, but her look was fierce. I went.

We all sat around the little table in the staff room. Mr. Lemsky rubbed one hand over his face and sighed. "I'm really sorry about this, Digby. This article is nothing but nonsense. I would have stopped it from going to print—I should have stopped it from going to print—but I was getting a root canal yesterday when the paper was sent out for printing. I had already scanned all the content for this edition. Then Nate told me he wanted to run a story about park renewal. That sounded safe to me, so I told him to go ahead. I didn't look into things more closely. I'm sorry, Digby. I've told Nate he can't work at the paper anymore for his co-op term."

Digby looked pained. "Don't fire Nate, Mr. Lemsky. Not because of me."

"I had to, Digby. He knew what he was doing was wrong. He had no facts to go on. He just wanted an exciting story. That's not how it's done. You can't make things up or print things without people's permission."

"But I told him he could take my picture."

"Did he tell you what he was going to do with it?"

Digby shook his head.

"Did you claim the winning lottery ticket?"

"Claim it? Like, tell official people I have the winning numbers?"

"Yes."

Digby shook his head again. "No."

"Are you planning to renew Oakview Park?"

"How do you mean?"

"Buy new playground equipment, redo the landscaping, stuff like that."

"No. That's not my plan."

"Well, you see? You can't print what's not true. I'm sorry this happened. So far it looks like you're getting a lot of good-natured attention from the story and that's about it. I hope no harm comes from it. Do you have any questions for me before I go?"

"Yes." Digby looked intently at Mr. Lemsky. "What's a root canal?"

Mr. Lemsky smiled. "Something that's not a whole lot of fun. Can't say I recommend it. But we can talk about that another day." He stood up and shook Digby's hand. He shook mine too. He stopped and talked to Cheryl before he left.

"Are you going to send Digby to do something out back so he can get away from this craziness?" I asked Cheryl when Mr. Lemsky had gone.

"No, I'm going to do one better than that." Cheryl whistled loudly to get everyone's attention. "All right, everybody," she said. "The paper got it wrong.

End of story. Leave Digby alone now. I'm closing up early. Everybody go home." People grumbled while they folded up their papers and brought their mugs to the counter, but soon the shop was empty. We cleaned things up and turned off the lights.

"You all right, hon?" Cheryl asked Digby as we zipped up our coats and walked toward the door.

"Sure, Cheryl. I'm getting home early. That means I can play some foosball and maybe watch some TV. I'll see you tomorrow. Bye, Skye! Hey, I like that. It rhymes."

"It sure does. See you, Digby."

Cheryl and I stood on the sidewalk for a minute, watching Digby walk away. When he was gone from view, Cheryl looked at me. "They'll forget about it soon enough," she said.

Chapter Nine

Cheryl was right. Over the next couple of days, everybody in Kentville stopped talking about the newspaper article and the lottery. Just before closing on Thursday, Digby told me he was going to restock the shelves in the back. "You okay out here, Skye?" he asked me.

"I'm okay."

"You'll wipe the tables down?"

"I'll wipe the tables down."

"Good. I got my earbuds in, okay?"

"What are you listening to?" I asked, but Digby already had his earbuds in. As I was putting the last of the mugs into the dishwasher, I started thinking again about ways I could spend a million dollars. It had become a bit of a hobby of mine. Cheryl and Denny had said they were going to see a movie this evening. With a million dollars to spend, I could buy a lifetime supply of movie tickets. Maybe I could buy the whole theater for myself. Or I could build one in my new mansion and see movies with my friends whenever I wanted. Except...hmmm. I might have to buy some friends as well. I sighed. Maybe I could buy a boat and sail to an exotic island. Or I could buy an island and live there...by myself?

I had wiped down all the tables and was finishing the counters when the bells on the door tinkled. A woman came in. She looked to be in her forties. When she pushed off the hood to her black parka, I saw she had shoulder-length hair that had once been blond but was fading to gray.

She came up to the counter.

"Coffee?" I asked.

"Please." Her voice was low. "Small. Black."

"Is takeout okay? We're just closing up."

"Oh. Sure."

Digby didn't come back behind the counter, so I knew he hadn't heard her come in. I poured the coffee myself and punched the code into the cash register. "Anything else? Doughnut? Butter tart? They were made fresh today."

She shook her head and leaned toward the counter. "I'm Leann. Leann Jones?"

She said it like it was a question I should have the answer to. The name should have set off all kinds of alarm bells in my head, but for some reason it didn't register at first. Not until I handed her the cup of coffee and she said, "I'm looking for Digby. Digby Jones?"

Wait! Had she really said Leann? Leann Jones? This was Digby's mom? No way. She couldn't be. Could she? Digby's mom was dead. Wasn't she? She'd been killed in a motorcycle accident years ago. Cheryl had told me. A shiver went up my spine. What was going on? Was this good news or bad? Either Digby was about to get lucky all over again, or his life had just got a whole lot more complicated. I shook my head, trying to think things through. "Ah, he's not here right now." I probably should have said I didn't know anybody named Digby, but it was too late for that now.

The woman sighed. She looked up at the ceiling for a moment before speaking again. "I'd like to talk to him. Do you know where he lives?"

"No." I knew Digby lived in a group home close by, but I didn't know exactly where. Even if I did, I was pretty sure I shouldn't be handing out that information to someone I didn't know.

"Will he be in tomorrow?"

"Ah, I'm not in charge of the schedule, but you could check back in the morning."

"Okay." She laid some coins on the counter. "Thanks for the coffee."

Leann, if that's who she was, turned, took another slow look around the seating area and then walked out of the shop. As soon as she was gone, I ran to flip the *Open* sign to *Closed* and locked the front door. I hurried back behind the counter and stared at the money she had left. Leann Jones. Had I done the right thing in not calling Digby out front? Something had stopped me. Maybe it had bought us some time. I dumped the money in the cash-register drawer and hurried to the back. Digby was pulling stacks of paper cups out of boxes and putting them neatly on the shelves.

"Digby?"

He pulled an earbud away from one ear. "Hey, Skye."

"Are you okay?"

"Of course. I know how to stack cups. I've done it lots of times."

"No, I...did you...we just had a customer."

"Do you need me to fill the order?"

"No, I did it. But I—"

"Was it takeout?"

"Yes."

"Did you put a lid on the coffee cup?"

"Yes."

"Did you say, 'Have a nice day'?"

"Yes, no...I don't remember."

He frowned. "Did you wipe down the tables?"

"Yes. Digby, I need to tell you—"

Digby's forehead crinkled. "I can't talk now, Skye. I'm busy."

"But..."

Digby shook his head. I knew I wasn't going to be able to take this conversation any further. I wasn't sure just where to take it anyway. I tried calling Cheryl. The call went straight to voice mail.

I remembered again that she and Denny were at a movie. I didn't leave a message. What was I supposed to say?

Digby finished up out back. I finished up out front. Then we turned out the lights and went outside. I was afraid the woman might be waiting for him, but I didn't see her anywhere. Digby turned to walk home. "Bye, Skye. That rhymes. See you tomorrow."

My house was totally in the other direction. I took a few steps and then turned around. "Hey, Digby," I called. "Do you mind if I walk with you a little ways?"

He grinned. "Sure. Come on."

When we got to Digby's front door, everything seemed okay. There were no cars parked outside. "Do you want to watch some TV with me?" he asked.

"No, I think I'd better go home."

"You got homework?"

"Yeah. Some."

"Okay, see you tomorrow."

"You bet." I didn't know quite what to make of this new situation, but I did know one thing for sure. The next morning I wasn't going to school. I was going to the *Brew-n-Bake*.

Chapter Ten

When I got to the shop at eight, there was a small gray car parked out front. It had Ontario license plates. I peeked inside. On the back seat there was a copy of the *Register*. The one with Digby's picture on the front page. I figured that was how Leann knew where to start looking for Digby. She knew about the *Brew-n-Bake*. Thanks to blabbermouth Nate, she also knew about the money.

Leann was already inside, talking to Cheryl. I made my way quietly over to the counter. There was a group of four older guys drinking coffee and eating honey crullers at one of the tables by the window. They were talking about the hockey game the night before. They certainly wouldn't be overhearing the conversation at the counter. Neither would the young mom who was trying to get her wailing toddler to eat one of Denny's blueberry muffins. Try it, kiddo, I thought. You'll like it. But he just kept kicking, wanting to be set free from his stroller.

"Pardon the way this sounds," Cheryl was saying, "but I thought you were...I thought you had... Joey told Digby you were killed in an accident. How is it that you're on the other side of my counter then?"

Yeah, that was exactly what I wanted to know.

Leann looked down at her shoes. "I suspect Joey told Digby that so he wouldn't feel like I ran out on him."

"And did you?" Cheryl's voice was firm.

"Did I what?"

"Run out on him?"

"No, I just…it took me a long time to get my life together."

"And now?"

Leann drew herself up straighter and taller and looked Cheryl in the eye. "Now I'm back. And I want to have Digby with me. I want to get him out of that group home."

Shoot. She knew about the group home. "What if he likes it there?" I blurted. The two women turned to look at me. I shrugged. "They have foosball. And Ping-Pong."

"School holiday, Skye?" asked Cheryl.

I nodded. Something like that. Never mind that I was the one who had called it.

Cheryl turned back to Leann. She sighed. "Look,

I'm sorry if we don't sound particularly welcoming, but there's something you have to understand. We all love Digby. The whole town does. Nobody wants to see him hurt."

"I wouldn't hurt him. I'm his mother."

"You left him."

"I left him with two of the sweetest people on earth. I knew Joey and Amy would look after him. Better than I could have at the time. And they did, didn't they? But now they're gone. Digby's my boy. I'd like to see him."

"He probably won't remember you."

"You're right. He won't. I understand that. I'm counting on it actually. But that's okay. We can start over."

Cheryl took a deep breath and let it out again. "Okay, well, Digby's—"

No! I didn't like this. Maybe this lady was who she said she was, or maybe she just knew about

Joey and Amy and the group home because she'd done some research. I had the same bad feeling I'd had when Nate asked to take Digby's picture. I moved in beside Cheryl. "Have you got any ID?"

"Skye! For goodness' sake. What's come over you?" Cheryl asked.

But Cheryl didn't know the whole story. She didn't know Digby actually had that winning ticket. I didn't want to get between Digby and his mother, but I didn't want anyone taking advantage of him either. "That's a simple thing to ask for, don't you think?"

Cheryl looked back at Leann. "Well?"

Leann shrugged. "You may not believe this, but it turns out I don't have any on me. My bag was stolen at one of the service centers along the highway on my way east. That's the kind of luck I have, I guess." She smiled weakly. "I'm already working on getting my driver's license and credit cards replaced."

Cheryl considered this news. "Well, as I was

going to say…Digby's not coming in today anyway," she lied. "How about you get that ID back. Or maybe come in with someone who remembers you. Then we'll plan a nice little reunion. But it will be up to Digby. I'm not going to force anything."

"Of course. Thanks for everything." Leann zipped up her coat, pulled on her gloves and left.

Cheryl watched her get into the gray car. "What is that woman coming around here for now?" she muttered. "She's going to turn Digby's life upside down."

I knew a really good reason why Digby's mother might suddenly have appeared out of the woodwork. She wanted the new car a million dollars would buy her. She wanted the jewelry, the trips, the lifetime supply of Swedish Berries, and I bet she wouldn't say no to a private movie theater either. But I didn't say anything. The million dollars was Digby's news.

Cheryl looked at me closely. "You knew she was coming, didn't you?"

I nodded. "She came in last night."

Cheryl nodded. "I need to go do some thinking. If you don't have school today, how about putting in some extra time? Here come the quilting ladies for their tea and scones. I think Denny's got some cooling out back."

Chapter Eleven

I worked all morning. I served hot coffee, iced coffee and a dozen different flavors of tea. We sold out of scones and raspberry tarts, and I refilled the trays with coconut bars and cinnamon doughnuts just before Digby came in. Cheryl sent Digby to the back room. She told Denny to come up front for a while and run the counter. She told me to come with her to tell Digby what was going on.

"Me?"

"You're his friend, aren't you, Skye? Otherwise just what are you doing here today instead of being at school?"

Good question. I felt my cheeks burn a little as I followed her to the staff room.

Digby was sitting behind the small table. "Skye, you're here early!" he said when he saw me. "It's going to be a good day!"

"Digby," said Cheryl as she sat down across from him. She nodded at me to take the seat beside him. "I have something important to tell you."

His eyes got big. "I bet I'm getting a raise. And Skye is too. Is that why we're both here at this meeting?"

"A raise?" Cheryl chuckled. "No, that's not what I wanted to talk about."

"Oh. Aren't we doing a good job, Cheryl?"

"Yes, you're doing a good job, Digby. You too, Skye, but…" Cheryl shook her head and tried to refocus.

She took a deep breath. "Listen, Digs. There's a lady who came around this morning. She says…" Cheryl stopped and cleared her throat. "She says her name is Leann and that she's your mother."

"My mother?"

"Yes."

"Here?"

"Yes."

"My mother's name was Leann."

"I know, hon."

"But she died a long time ago."

"Well, maybe not. Maybe she was…lost."

"Lost?"

"And now she's found her way back."

"My mother?"

"Yes, hon."

"Here in Kentville?"

"She wants to see you."

"My mother?"

"Yes, Digby, she'd like to talk to you."

"My mother died a long time ago."

Cheryl sighed. She put a hand on Digby's. "Listen, Digby. Your mother…Leann…she would like to see you. What do you think about that? Isn't that pretty awesome? Isn't that exciting?"

He shook his head. "It's kind of weird."

That's what I thought.

"I know, Digs. Now I want you to understand that you do not have to do anything you don't want to do. You also should not go anywhere with anyone you don't want to. But it would probably be good to meet with this lady, don't you think? Me and Denny and Skye, we're all here for you, okay? We'll work with you to figure this out—if you need any help."

"Okay. But I think I'm good."

"Digby, do you understand what I'm telling you?"

He nodded. "My mother is here, and you want me to meet with her. Is she here right now?"

"No. We'll let you know when she's coming in."

"Oh. Then can I go to work now?"

"Sure, bud."

He grinned as he stood up and pushed in his chair. "I got to go. There's coffee to pour. Denny doesn't do it right."

"Nobody does it like you, Digby." Cheryl laughed as she watched him go. Then she looked over at me and shrugged. "He didn't fall to pieces like I thought he would. Do you think he gets what we're telling him?

"I don't think I get what we're telling him."

"Help me keep an eye on things, will you, Skye?"

"Sure. Do you think she's telling the truth, Cheryl?"

"What do you mean?"

"Do you think Leann's actually who she says she is?"

"Why would anyone come in claiming to be his mother if she wasn't actually his mother?"

"What about the article in the paper saying he—"

"That little piece in the *Register*? Nobody reads that. And that was just a bunch of baloney anyway."

"But—"

"Cheryl?" Digby hurried back over to where we were sitting. "Denny says he needs me to count the chocolate-chip cookies. Now. Right away. And he says he needs you out front."

Cheryl made a face. "What on earth is that man talking about? Count the…what? We don't—"

I had gone to the doorway and understood right away what Denny was up to. I waved at Cheryl to join me. Once she did, she called over her shoulder for Digby to start counting. "You better count them two or three times so we know exactly how many there are, okay, Digby? It's important."

"I'm on it! I've got my gloves on."

"Okay. Good." She pulled me out to the counter with her.

Leann was back.

She was with a guy who swore she was the Leann Jones who'd left Kentville fifteen years earlier. "I'd know her anywhere," he said. "There were a bunch of us who were friends back then. We had some great times."

"You're sure?"

"Absolutely."

Cheryl thought for a moment. "Okay. Why don't you come back at five thirty, Leann? That's just before closing. The shop shouldn't be too busy then. I'll make sure Digby's here."

Leann smiled. "Perfect."

Cheryl, Denny and I all stared after them when Leann and her friend left the shop. Could we trust her? Could we trust him?

"Do you know him, Cheryl?"

"No, but I don't know everyone in town yet. We came up from Halifax, remember?"

"He had ID saying he was who he said he was," said Denny.

"That tells us who he is. But it doesn't tell us how he knows Leann." Cheryl sighed. "I guess we'll see what happens this afternoon. No use worrying about things until then."

But I couldn't stop worrying about it. There had to be a way to find out if this really was Digby's mother. To prove things one way or the other. What was it? I just had a bad feeling about this whole thing. It was bubbling inside me and making me feel weird. I needed an answer.

"Two hundred and six," said Digby at my side.

"What?"

"Chocolate-chip cookies."

"Oh." I looked up at him. "Good."

"I think so anyway. I had to count them so many times. There were more, but I ate a couple. I hate doing things with numbers."

Chapter Twelve

Leann walked in at five twenty-five. She was alone. She smiled over at us and took a seat at a table for four near the windows. Cheryl quickly packed up the dozen doughnuts Todd Matthews had asked for and sent him out the door with it. Then she asked me to go sit with Leann while she went to get some coffee and brownies. And Digby.

"Mmm. Brownies. I love them," Leann said as I took the chair next to her.

"Just like Joey, huh?"

She raised one eyebrow. "What?"

"Uncle Joey. Digby told me he loved chocolate too."

"Oh, right."

"Digby told me Joey used to bring chocolate and flowers to Amy every year on their anniversary."

"Yeah, he was sweet that way."

"When was that again?"

"When was what?"

"Their anniversary. I can't remember when Digby said it was."

Leann stared up at the ceiling, just like Digby did when he was thinking about something. That was a good sign. Now say April 28, I thought. Then I'll know for sure that you are who you say you are and my insides can stop twisting themselves in knots.

"Hmmm. I don't remember. I've never been good with dates."

Rats. That didn't tell me anything. Digby had said that even his uncle Joey had trouble remembering his anniversary. Digby would be coming out here soon, and I still didn't know what I needed to know. What now?

Leann looked over behind the counter. She cleared her throat. "Is Digby here? I thought you said five thirty."

"Sure, Digby—" I stopped. I got really warm. My head prickled under my hat. I worked hard to keep the excitement from showing on my face. I'd suddenly realized exactly what I needed to ask Leann. I took a deep breath and smiled. I tried to make my voice come out normal. "Digby—that's such a great name. How did you end up choosing it?"

Leann smiled. "It is nice, isn't it? Where did I come up with it?" She shrugged. "Oh, I don't know.

Jones is such a common last name. I knew I'd have to give my little boy a really special first name to go with it."

I nodded. "It *is* special. It suits him. So he's not, uhhh....named after anyone?"

"No." Leann shook her head and laughed. "He's just Digby. I thought it was a unique name. Something just for him. I don't go in much for tradition, naming kids after people they never even knew. You know what I'm saying?"

I nodded. Oh yeah, lady, I thought. I know exactly what you're saying. Her answer had told me exactly what I needed to know. But how was I going to tell the others that this Leann Jones was a fraud?

Chapter Thirteen

Cheryl was making her way back with a full tray when Jordy McDonald pushed through the door, making the bells jump and jingle. No Digby yet. I wasn't sure what I should do next. What should I say? How should I say it? Who should I say it to? All these questions were giving me a headache. But I needed to make a decision, fast.

Jordy was delivering the half dozen *Registers* Cheryl always got for the customers to read over coffee. He waved one around and crowed that there was big news.

"What news?" asked Cheryl.

"Somebody claimed the ticket."

"What ticket?" asked Leann, reaching for the coffee Cheryl was holding out to her.

"The million-dollar ticket, of course." He slapped the paper down on the table. "A trucker from Newfoundland bought it here when he was passing through."

The million-dollar ticket? A trucker from Newfoundland? Digby's ticket? No way. I jumped up, accidentally knocking over Leann's coffee. I didn't have time to apologize. I ran to the back to find Digby.

I almost crashed into him as he was coming out of the bathroom. "Digby! Where's your lottery ticket?"

"In my wallet where Uncle Joey told me to keep it. Why? What's the matter, Skye?"

My heart was pounding. "Somebody just claimed it."

He shook his head. "That's not right. Unless there were two tickets with the same numbers? Could there be two winning tickets, Skye?"

"Where's the ticket, Digby?"

He dug his wallet out of his back pocket and pulled out the ticket. "Here it is. Look. Ten, twenty-one, four, twenty-eight, seven, sixteen. Those are the numbers, right? Unless..." Digby licked his thumb and very carefully started rubbing away the chocolate smudge. Then he stopped. He stared.

"What is it, Digby? What are you looking at? What do you see?"

Digby looked up at me. He turned the ticket so I could see it. The final number was not a six. It was an eight. It was not the winning ticket after all. *Oh no.* Digby leaned back against the wall and slowly slid down to the floor. He held the ticket tight against his chest. His face just seemed to melt, and he began to cry. Big, heaving sobs.

My throat got tight. "Digby, hey, it's okay. It was a lot of money, but you'll be okay. You still have your job and…"

He shook his head. "No. No, Skye."

I crouched down beside him. "Yes, Digby. You'll be okay. If you need money or—"

"It's not the money. It's not the money."

"Why are you upset then?"

"I'm not upset."

"You sound upset."

He took in a ragged breath and shook his head. "I'm not upset. I'm happy. I'm very, very happy."

"You're happy?" I thought about that for a moment. "Why are you happy?"

"Don't you see? Uncle Joey picked the number eighteen. Not sixteen. Eighteen. He picked *my* birthday as one of his favorite numbers. Uncle Joey is the best uncle in the world. But he's, he's…I miss him." Digby started sobbing all over again.

I grabbed some napkins from an open package on one of the shelves and sat down on the floor beside him. "Here, Digby. It's okay. It's going to be okay." He took the napkins I held out to him and blew his nose.

Cheryl appeared in the doorway. "What's— Digby, are you all right? What on earth happened?"

Digby looked up. "Oh," he said, taking a deep breath. "Oh no, Cheryl, I forgot. I need to come out front. You asked me to come out front and meet my mother at five thirty." He wiped his face. He stood up. He tucked in his shirt and straightened his visor.

Cheryl shook her head. "Hold tight there, bud. I don't know exactly what's going on, but Leann's not out there right now." She frowned. "She was out there, but now she's gone."

I looked toward the seating area. Gone? Of course she was gone.

"Where did she go?" asked Digby.

"I don't know. I went to get a cloth to clean things up after Skye knocked Leann's coffee flying. While I was at the sink, she disappeared."

"She's gone? But I didn't even get to meet her."

And he never would. I knew it. When Leann found out the winning ticket belonged to someone else, she was no longer interested in meeting Digby Jones. I felt so sorry for Digby at that moment—the moment he lost everything all over again. I reached over and put my hand on his arm. "Digby, I'm sorry," I said softly. "I'm really sorry, but I need to tell you something."

He had been staring at the doorway he was supposed to walk through to find his mother. He looked at Cheryl for a moment, then focused on me. "What, Skye? What do you need to tell me?"

"I don't know exactly how to say this, but…your mother—"

Digby was looking at me so intently it almost hurt. "My mother. She died a long time ago."

I took a deep breath. "Yes. So that woman... Leann. Whoever she is, she is not your mom."

"Wait...Skye, how do you know that for certain?" asked Cheryl. "Digby, we'll try to find her. We'll find out where she went, and we'll get this all straightened out."

"It already is straightened out, Cheryl. I asked her how Digby got his name."

"What do you mean?"

"About the grandpa named John and being born in Digby. She didn't know. She said she wanted to come up with a unique name to go with Jones."

"You asked her about his name. That's brilliant! Why didn't I think of that?"

"There's no way she's your mother, Digby."

Digby put his hand over mine and patted it. "I already knew that, Skye."

"Hold on," said Cheryl. She set her hands on her hips. "What do you mean you already knew that? Why did you say you'd come meet her then?"

"You asked me to. You said my mother was here and she wanted to talk to me. But she's not my mom."

"Right. But Digs," asked Cheryl, "how did you *know* she isn't your mom?"

He cocked his head. "Simple. Uncle Joey told me my mom died a long time ago. Uncle Joey would never lie to me."

"You're right," said Cheryl. She shook her head. "Simple."

Chapter Fourteen

Cheryl said she'd walk Digby home after we closed up the *Brew-n-Bake* at six. She told me she wanted to let the workers at the group home know what had been going on. In case Leann was still around.

"You want to play some Ping-Pong with me, Cheryl?" asked Digby.

"You know, I think that might be just what I need, bud. It's been a tough day."

"Do your feet hurt? We can watch TV instead."

Cheryl laughed. "They always hurt, Digby. Let's go."

"Bye, Skye," called Digby as they set out down the sidewalk. "See you next week. It's going to be a great one."

"See you Monday," I called after them. I smiled and shook my head. Digby always saw the bright side of everything. How did he do that? I started walking home. There was the smallest hint of spring in the breeze. I took off my hat and let the wind tease my hair.

The house was empty when I got home. Creaky as ever. I had planned to go up to my room as usual. But as I walked through the kitchen, I got this sudden urge to bake brownies. They didn't turn out as good as Denny's, but they smelled great. Then I got the idea to wait up and share them with my mom when she came in. I tidied up the kitchen. I threw in a load of laundry so I would have a clean supply of black outfits for the next week. Then I watched some YouTube videos at the table until I heard her key in the door.

"Hi, Mom."

She jumped. "Oh, hey, Skye. What's…hey, it smells good in here." She looked at the plate of brownies on the counter. "Mmmm. What's the occasion?"

I shrugged. "No occasion. Do you ever need an occasion to eat brownies?"

"Nope," she said, reaching for the plate.

"I was just in the mood for chocolate," I said. But I didn't tell her why. I didn't say that I'd made brownies because I was thinking about people who loved chocolate. That I was thinking about how important some people were to other people. That I was thinking about moms and how lucky I was to have mine. Even if I was mad at her because she had dragged me halfway across the country. I didn't tell her that there was something I had missed thinking about until now. Why had my mom dragged me halfway across the country? Why had she taken me with her to Kentville? She needed me. She knew I needed her. And she was right. I did. I didn't tell her any of that. But I knew it.

Mom told me a bit about her shift. Then she said she was going to flop on the couch and watch a movie. "You want to watch with me, Skye?" she asked. "I know it's late, but there's no school tomorrow."

I hesitated. I was tired and used to hanging out in my room. But she looked so hopeful. "Sure," I said. I followed her into the living room. The floor groaned under my feet. "Hey, Mom, do you think it would be cool if we had our own movie theater?"

"Very cool."

"What would you buy if you had a million dollars?"

"A million dollars?"

"If you could pick anything?"

"Well, let's see, where should I start? I bet you have some ideas."

I laughed. "I might. You go first."

The next morning I slept in. Then I did my homework. The math was easy. The English assignment, which I had been putting off, was to write a short story. I thought for a while. I pulled out the notebooks I had scribbled in the backs of before I'd started working at the *Brew-n-Bake*. Then I started typing. When I looked up again, a couple of hours had gone by. When I finished, I went to find the leftover brownies.

At school on Monday, Lainey waved at me again at lunch. I had planned to go to the library but decided to sit with her instead. Lainey introduced me to a couple of the other kids at the table. They seemed nice.

When I got to work that afternoon, the first thing Digby said to me was, "Don't ask me how I am.

Cheryl already asked me one thousand times today. I'm fine. Why wouldn't I be fine? I won the foosball tournament yesterday afternoon. I get to work at my favorite place today. Denny made apple fritters and strawberry-filled doughnuts. Olivia came in, and I gave her one. I said 'on the house' and she said that made her day. Mrs. Kerrigan told me she has new twin grandsons. We're having spaghetti at the group home tonight. I'm fine. Life is good."

And I agreed. Life did feel a little better. The next day, however, Mr. Everett, my English teacher, asked me to come to his classroom at lunch. *Uh-oh.* I wondered when the no-homework thing was going to catch up to me. Even though I had handed in the latest assignment, there were quite a few I hadn't. I was probably going to get detention or something.

Mr. Everett was sitting at his desk when I walked in. He was eating an apple. And reading something. He motioned for me to sit in a desk in the front row. He smiled. "So, Skye, how's it going?"

I shrugged.

"Fitting in okay?"

"Sure."

"I haven't seen a lot of work from you."

Here it comes, I thought. I felt a little warm.

"But I wasn't worried. I thought you probably just needed a little time. Moving and starting at a new school can be tough."

I didn't say anything.

"I'm glad I waited." He tapped the papers in his hand. "I read your story, Skye. It's good. Really good. So good that I want to talk to you about something. I heard about this writing contest for high school students. I just put the poster up on the bulletin board this morning. I think you should send this in."

"Me?" I squeaked.

"Yes. "

"You want me to send in my story?"

"Yes. You may want to make a few small changes, but—"

"To a writing contest?"

"Yes."

"Wowzers."

He laughed. "Is that a yes?"

The next day I was lying on my bed, revising my story for the contest, when Cade called. "Hey, Nerd Girl. How's it going? I miss you."

I almost dropped the phone. He missed me? I thought my brother had forgotten all about me. At first the lump in my throat was so big I couldn't talk at all. But soon I found I couldn't stop. I told him everything. About the coffee shop. About Digby. About the writing contest. Everything.

"Whoa, you have a lot going on," he said. "But you're doing okay?"

I thought for a minute. "I think so."

"Good. Me too. Just busy. Send me a picture, okay? I'll call again next week, if you think that's cool."

"It's cool."

I sat back against the wall, took a picture and sent it to him.

He immediately texted back.

What did you do to your hair???????

Oh yeah. I forgot he hadn't seen the new me yet.

You don't like it?

It's different.

And?

I guess sometimes different is ok.

This time?

I think so. Yeah.

I thought so too.

On Thursday Mr. Lemsky came into the *Brew-n-Bake.* "Hey, Mr. Lemsky," called Digby.

"Hello, Digby."

Digby handed him a mug of steaming black coffee and a butter tart. Mr. Lemsky smiled. "Now how did you know I was in the mood for a butter tart?"

Digby beamed. "I could see it. I could just see you're having a butter tart kind of day."

"You're absolutely right, Digby. I'll take that recommendation." Mr. Lemsky pulled out his wallet to pay for his coffee and tart. "Skye," he said, "while we're on the topic of recommendations, Digby tells me you have a way with words. I wonder if you would consider volunteering at the *Register*. We need someone to cover events on weekends now and then. We've already got one other young lady who helps with that. Lainey Cross. Do you know her?"

I smiled. "I know Lainey."

"Of course, you should check this with your mother first."

I smiled again. I already knew what she would say about it.

Wow! What a week. Inspired by all the unexpected things that had been happening, on Friday I did something totally wild. I wore my green Brew-n-Bake shirt instead of the black one. But I kept the hat. Cheryl was on her way out when I went into the staff room to drop my backpack and hang up my coat. She stopped at the door. "It's been busy today, Skye. Denny just put some Nanaimo bars in the fridge. They should be ready in about an hour if you need them."

"Okay," I said.

Cheryl looked me up and down. She smiled. "Laundry day today?"

I shrugged. "Something like that."

"Look what I'm wearing," she said. "I got a brand-new pair of super-comfy shoes from Digby this morning. That kid is a gem. How did he know my feet hurt?"

I laughed. All of Kentville knew Cheryl's feet hurt. That could have gone into the *Register* as fact.

"Hey, Digby," I said when I got out front.

He was busy checking the stir-stick containers and held up one hand. When he was done, he said, "Hey, Skye. After you crawl out of your cave tomorrow morning, do you want to meet me at Oakview Park? I have something I want to show you. It's a surprise."

I adjusted my green shirt. It was so new, it was still a little stiff. I tugged down on my hat. "Sure," I said. But, after everything that had happened already this week, I figured nothing could surprise me. Of course, I was wrong.

Chapter Fifteen

When I got to the park, Digby was already there, sitting on a bench under a tree with no leaves on it. I shivered as I sat down beside him. "This would be nicer in May," I said. "It does get warmer here in May, doesn't it?"

"Of course it does. Kentville is the best place in the world in May," said Digby. "Here, I have something for you."

"For me? You didn't have to do that."

"I know. I wanted to."

I took off my mittens to unwrap the package he gave me. Inside was a notebook. The cover was a beautiful soft leather, and every page was empty. Waiting.

"It's to write all your great words in."

I couldn't talk for a moment.

"Don't you like it?" asked Digby. "I could get you a sweater instead. Or a puzzle."

"I love it, Digby. It's perfect. Thank you."

He grinned. His eyes were bright, and his cheeks were pink from the cold. "I got it and Cheryl's shoes with the rest of the money left over after I bought all the things on my list. Plus, I got two new sets of Ping-Pong paddles. The ones at the group home all have dings in them. Sometimes Manuel hits the table when he's trying to serve. Well, sometimes I do that too."

I laughed. Then I thought for a moment. "Wait, what list do you mean, Digby?"

"The list you helped me make. Of how to spend my money."

"But you don't have any money!"

"Yes I do."

"No, Digby. Somebody else had the winning ticket. Remember?"

"I know. But that doesn't have anything to do with my list. I got a whole pile of money from Uncle Joey and Aunt Amy. Aunt Amy was always really good with money. She wrote down how she wanted to give a certain amount away, and she wrote down that Digby, that's me, should choose where the money should go. So I did."

I felt a little bit of panic rising in my chest. Digby had said himself that he was not good with numbers. "And you...you already gave that money away? How did you—"

"Mr. Simms helped me."

"Mr. Simms?" My spidey senses kicked in hard. Who was Mr. Simms? Could Digby trust him? After Nate and then Leann…

"He's my financial adviser."

Again it took me a moment before I could respond. "Your what?"

"My financial adviser. He helps me with money stuff. Aunt Amy set us up."

"You have a financial adviser?"

"Doesn't everybody?"

I was totally, completely, 100 percent gobsmacked. There was no other word for it. "So you got the plane ticket for Mrs. Lee?"

Digby nodded excitedly. "She leaves July 3."

"And the bike?"

"Well, the gift card, like you said."

"And the stove?"

"It was delivered to the soup kitchen yesterday."

"What about the roof?"

"Mr. Todd Matthews of Matthews' Roofing and Siding went to see the Dubrovskys, and he put the job in his calendar for April."

"That's amazing, Digby."

"I know. April is only, like, a month from now."

"No, I mean…you chose well."

"You think Aunt Amy would be happy?"

"Very happy."

We were quiet for a moment. Then I turned to him and said, "Digby, do you know why I think you grew so big?"

"Fruits and vegetables? I always try to eat them, although I don't like carrots."

"Not even in those supersize carrot muffins Denny makes?"

"No. But don't tell. Every time Denny gives me one, I give it away."

I laughed.

"Uncle Joey used to say his favorite vegetable was potato chips, but Aunt Amy always rolled her eyes and said, 'Now Digby, we all know that's not a vegetable, don't we. Eat your peas.' And I did. I like peas."

"Hmmm. Me too. But I mean something different, Digby. I think you grew so big because otherwise your heart wouldn't fit inside. You're a really good guy, Digby Jones. Your aunt and uncle would be super proud of you." I looked him in the eye. "You believe me, don't you?"

"You're my friend, Skye. You would never lie to me. Just like…"

Digby's lip quivered just a little, and I knew it probably wasn't just from him shivering in the frosty air. He was thinking about his uncle Joey. I gave him a minute, then tried to change the subject.

"Hey, Digby. I forgot something. What about the $1,500 surprise?"

A slow smile spread across Digby's face. His eyes twinkled. "I got that too."

"What is it? Wasn't it something for the park?" I scanned the playground. There was no sign of a skate park. The slides and swings looked as ancient as ever.

"You're sitting on it."

"What?"

"You're sitting on it. Look." Digby shifted over to reveal a shiny brass plaque that read *In memory of Joey and Amy Jones.*

"You bought them this bench."

"Yep. And I put their names on it. They liked to come here and sit at one of the picnic tables, but Aunt Amy always said she wished there was a bench in the shade. Now there is."

"Now there is."

Sitting on that bench, looking out over a soggy playground, I felt I was seeing something I had not seen before. That I had learned something. No, that wasn't quite it. It was more than that. That I had won something.

"I'm glad I know you, Digby."

"Me too. I'm glad you came to Kentville, Skye. It's a really awesome place. And with you here, it's even better."

"Like a bench in the shade?"

"Like a bench in the shade."

I pulled my mittens back on and stood up. I felt kind of funny. Different. Whatever was bubbling around inside, it was giving me lots of energy. "I'd better get going. I have to cover a quilt show for Mr. Lemsky this afternoon. With Lainey."

"Say hi to the scones ladies."

"I will."

"I have to go too. Me and the other guys from the group home are going bowling."

"That sounds fun."

"Yeah. I hope I win."

I laughed. "Hey, Digby, you know what we have to do soon?"

"What?"

"We need to plan that day away in Halifax."

"Oh yeah!"

"I'll ask my mom if she can drive us. Maybe Lainey can come, and we can ask Cheryl what we should go see."

"Maybe she can come too. Her and Denny."

"Sure. Why not?" And I'll send pictures to Cade, I thought. And maybe even to Mel.

"And we can have dinner at KFC, right?"

"Absolutely." We did a clumsy mitten high five. "Thanks again for the notebook," I added.

"You're welcome. See you Monday?"

"See you Monday."

"Bye, Skye." I heard Digby chuckle as he walked away. "That rhymes."

Acknowledgments

Many thanks to Tanya Trafford and the marvelous team at Orca Books for bringing this story to shelves, to the teachers and librarians who make space for it, and to the readers who pick it up. Thanks also to my family for their steady encouragement and support and to all the wonderful people out there who make the world a brighter place just by being who they are.

Sylvia Taekema's first novel, *Seconds*, was voted a Silver Birch Express Award Honour Book. She is also the author of the middle-grade novel *Ripple Effect*, as well as *Running Behind* in the Orca Currents line. Sylvia lives in Muskoka, Ontario.

For more information on all the books

in the Orca Currents line, please visit

orcabook.com